Dear Parents and Educators,

Welcome to Penguin Young Readers! As parents and educators, you know that each child develops at their own pace—in terms of speech, critical thinking, and, of course, reading. Penguin Young Readers recognizes this fact. As a result, each Penguin Young Readers book is assigned a traditional easy-to-read level (1–4) as well as an F&P Text Level (A–P). Both of these systems will help you choose the right book for your child. Please refer to the back of each book for specific leveling information. Penguin Young Readers features esteemed authors and illustrators, stories about favorite characters, fascinating nonfiction, and more!

Mo Jackson: Get on the Ice, Mo!

LEVEL **3**

F&P TEXT
LEVEL **J**

This book is perfect for a **Transitional Reader** who:
- can read multisyllable and compound words;
- can read words with prefixes and suffixes;
- is able to identify story elements (beginning, middle, end, plot, setting, characters, problem, solution); and
- can understand different points of view.

Here are some **activities** you can do during and after reading this book:
- Adding -ing to words: One of the rules when adding -ing to words is, when a word ends with an -e, take off the -e and add -ing. With other words, you simply add the -ing ending to the root word. The following words are -ing words in this story. On a separate piece of paper, write down the root word for each word: helping, facing, skating, letting. Next, add -ing to the following words from the story: look, crash, get, put, take, walk, start.
- Summarize: Work with the child to write a short summary about what happened in the story. What happened in the beginning? What happened in the middle? What happened at the end?

Remember, sharing the love of reading with a child is the best gift you can give!

*This book has been officially leveled by using the F&P Text Level Gradient™ leveling system.

For my joyful grandson, Ari. —D. A .A.

For John Kutch, who taught us to skate. —S. R.

Penguin Young Readers
An imprint of Penguin Random House LLC
New York

First published in the United States of America by Penguin Young Readers,
an imprint of Penguin Random House LLC, 2022

Text copyright © 2022 by David Adler
Illustrations copyright © 2022 by Sam Ricks

Visit us online at penguinrandomhouse.com.

Library of Congress Cataloging-in-Publication Data is available.

Manufactured in Spain

ISBN 9780593352748

1 3 5 7 9 10 8 6 4 2

EST

G READERS

LEVEL 3
TRANSITIONAL READER

GET ON THE ICE, MO!

by David A. Adler
illustrated by Sam Ricks

"Skate to me,"

Mo's dad says.

"Skate to me."

"Wee!" Mo calls out.

He looks at his skates as

he slides across the ice.

CRASH!

"No, no," his dad tells him.

"Don't look down.

Look ahead."

Mo gets up.

He tries again.

CRASH!

He falls again.

"Hi, Mo."

"Hi, Amy.

My dad is helping me get

ready for the game."

"I'll help, too.

I need to practice."

Mo and Amy put on
their helmets.
They take their sticks
and skate.
Amy slides
across the ice.
She even skates
backward.

Mo skates and falls.

He gets up and tries again.

He falls again.

Amy tells him, "You don't look
at your feet when you walk.
Don't look at your feet
when you skate."

Amy drops a puck
on the ice.

She hits it to Mo.

Whoosh!

The puck hits Mo's stick
and bounces off.

It slides toward the net.

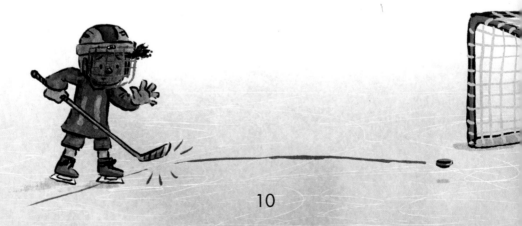

"Nice shot!" Amy calls out.

"But I didn't do anything!"

"Yes you did," Amy says.

She skates to Mo.

"Look at the bottom of your stick.

It's facing the net."

Mo moves his stick.

Now it's not facing the net.

Amy hits the puck to Mo.

It hits his stick and goes the

other way.

"Let's go!"

Coach Mimi calls to her team.

"Practice skating.

Practice hitting the puck."

Amy hits the puck to Mo.

He turns his stick just right.

The puck slides toward the goal.

Mo practices skating.

He skates across the ice.

He skates by Coach

Mimi and looks down.

CRASH!

Coach Mimi shakes

her head.

Coach Mimi calls Mo's
team together.
They are the Ducks.
"You will all get to play,
but only six at a time."

She tells the team who will start

the game.

"Max at goal.

Eve, Ben, Kate, Jane, and

of course Amy."

Amy is the best player on the team.

TWEET!

The game starts.

Amy is on the ice.

Mo is on the bench.

The puck slides quickly
across the ice.

It goes from the Ducks to the
other team, the Geese.

It goes from one player to another.

The puck comes to Amy, but
three players from the other team
are between her and the net.
"They are not letting Amy shoot
at the goal," Coach Mimi says.
"They are not letting her score!"

Amy passes the puck to Ben.

He swings his stick and hits

the puck, but he doesn't score.

TWEET!

It's the end of the first period.

"Let me play,"

Mo says to Coach Mimi.

"Amy will pass to me and I'll score."

Coach Mimi tells Mo,

"Everyone will play."

For the second period, she takes Ben out of the game and puts in Fran.

She takes out Kate and puts in Alan.

Mo is still on the bench.

The puck goes from the Ducks to
the Geese.

The teams don't score.

TWEET!

It's the end of the second period.

For the third period, Coach Mimi takes Alan out of the game and puts in Jay.

She takes out Jane and puts in Gary.

She doesn't take out Amy.

The game is almost over.

The coach takes out Eve
and puts in Mo.
She tells him,
"Don't look at your feet.
Don't fall."

Mo skates toward the net.

He does not look down.

The puck slides quickly across
the ice.

It goes from one player to another.

Mo stands off to the
side of the net.

Now Amy has the puck.

Three Geese are between
her and the net.

Mo stands alone.

The bottom of his stick is facing

the net.

Amy hits the puck.

Whoosh!

It hits Mo's stick and bounces off.

It slides into the net.

GOAL!

TWEET!

The game is over.

"MO! MO!" the Ducks
and Coach Mimi shout.

"You won the game!"

"Mo," his dad says.

"You did it."

"No, Amy did it," Mo says.

"She hit the puck just right."

"We did it together," Amy says,

"and we won."